W9-CPN-988

The Emperor and the Kite

The Emperor and the Kite

pictures by Ed Young

JANE YOLEN

COLLINS 🌳 WORLD / *CLEVELAND AND NEW YORK*

For my father, who is king of the kite fliers,
and
for my little princess, Heidi Elisabet

Published by William Collins+World Publishing Co., Inc.
2080 W. 117th Street, Cleveland, Ohio 44111
Published simultaneously in Canada by
Nelson, Foster & Scott Ltd.
Library of Congress catalog card number: 67-13816
ISBN #0-529-00255-8.
Text copyright © 1967 by Jane Yolen
Illustrations copyright © 1967 by The World Publishing Company
Typography by Jack Jaget

Once in ancient China there lived a princess who was the fourth daughter of the emperor. She was very tiny. In fact she was so tiny her name was Djeow Seow, which means "the smallest one." And, because she was so tiny, she was not thought very much of—when she was thought of at all.

Her brothers, who were all older and bigger and stronger than she,
were thought of all the time. And they were like four rising suns
in the eyes of their father. They helped the emperor rule the kingdom
and teach the people the ways of peace.

Even her three sisters were all older and bigger and stronger than she.
They were like three midnight moons in the eyes of their father.
They were the ones who brought food to his table.

But Djeow Seow was like a tiny star in the emperor's sight.
She was not even allowed to bring a grain of rice to the meal, so little
was she thought of. In fact she was so insignificant, the emperor
often forgot he had a fourth daughter at all.
And so, Djeow Seow ate by herself.
And she talked to herself.

And she played by herself, which was the loneliest thing of all.
Her favorite toy was a kite of paper and sticks.

Every morning, when the wind came from the east past the rising sun,
she flew her kite. And every evening, when the wind went to the west
past the setting sun, she flew her kite. Her toy was like a flower
in the sky. And it was like a prayer in the wind.

In fact a monk who passed the palace daily made up a poem about her kite.

> *My kite sails upward,*
> *Mounting to the high heavens.*
> *My soul goes on wings.*

But then, he was a monk, and given to such thoughts.
As for Princess Djeow Seow, she thanked him each day for his prayer.
Then she went back to flying her toy.

But all was not peaceful in the kingdom,
just as the wind is not always peaceful.
For the wind can trouble the waters of a still
pond. And there were evil men plotting against the emperor.

They crept up on him one day when he was alone, when his
four sons were away ruling in the furthermost parts of the kingdom
and his three daughters were down in the garden. And only
Princess Djeow Seow, so tiny she seemed part of the corner where she sat,
saw what happened.

The evil men took the emperor to a tower in the middle of a wide, treeless plain. The tower had only a single window, with an iron bar across the center. The plotters sealed the door with bricks and mortar once the emperor was inside.

Then they rode back to the palace and declared that the emperor was dead.

When his sons and daughters heard this, they all fled to a neighboring kingdom where they spent their time sobbing and sighing. But they did nothing else all day long.

All except Djeow Seow. She was so tiny, the evil men did not notice her at all. And so, she crept to the edge of the wide, treeless plain. And there she built a hut of twigs and branches.

Every day at dawn and again at dark,
she would walk across the plain to the tower.
And there she would sail her stick-and-paper kite.
To the kite string she tied a tiny basket
filled with rice and poppyseed cakes,
water chestnuts and green tea. The kite pulled the basket high,
high in the air, up as high as the window in the tower.
And, in this way, she kept her father alive.

So they lived for many days: the emperor in his tower
and the princess in a hut near the edge of the plain.
The evil men ruled with their cruel, harsh ways,
and the people of the country were very sad.

One day, as the princess prepared a basket of food for her father, the old monk passed by her hut. She smiled at him, but he seemed not to see her.

Yet, as he passed, he repeated his prayer in a loud voice. He said:

> *My kite sails upward,*
> *Mounting to the high heavens.*
> *My emperor goes on wings.*

The princess started to thank him. But then she stopped. Something
was different. The words were not quite right.
"Stop," she called to the monk. But he had already passed by. He was a monk,
after all, and did not take part in things of this world.

And then Djeow Seow understood. The monk was telling her something
important. And she understood.

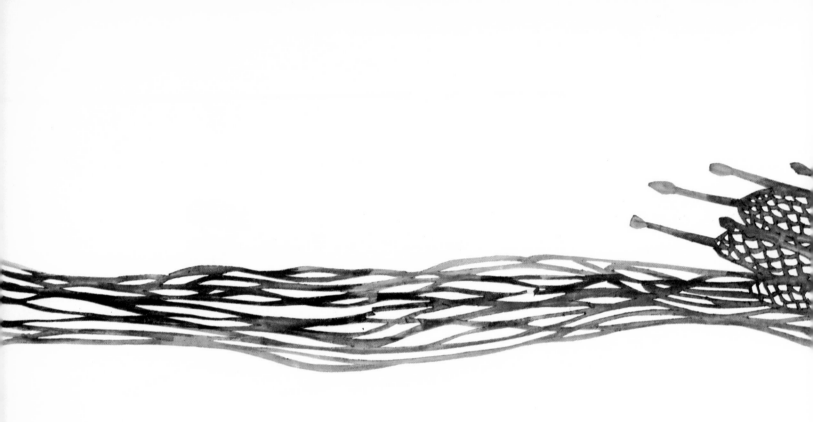

Each day after that, when she was not bringing food to her father,
Djeow Seow was busy. She twined a string of grass and vines, and wove in strands
of her own long black hair. When her rope was as thick as her waist
and as high as the tower, she was ready. She attached the

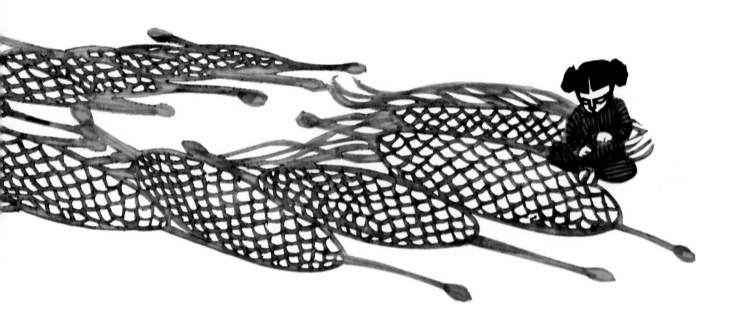

rope to the string of the stick-and-paper kite, and made her way
across the treeless plain.
When she reached the tower, she called to her father.
But her voice was as tiny as she, and her words were lost in the wind.

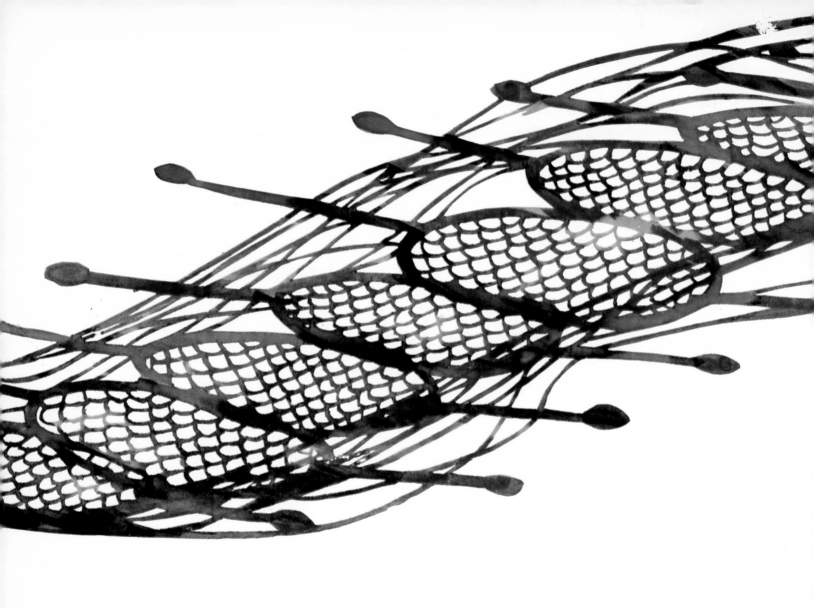

At last, though, the emperor looked out and saw his daughter flying her kite. He expected the tiny basket of food to sail up to his window as it had done each day. But what should he see but the strand of vines and grass and long black hair. The wind was raging above, holding the kite in its steely grip. And the princess was below, holding tight to the end of the rope.

Although the emperor had never really understood the worth of his tiniest daughter before, he did now. And he promised himself that if her plan worked she would never again want for anything, though all she had ever wanted was love. Then he leaned farther out of the tower window and grasped the heavy strand. He brought it into his tower room and loosened the string of the kite. He set the kite free, saying, "Go to thy home in the sky, great kite." And the kite flew off toward the heavens.

Then the emperor tied one end of the thick strand to the heavy iron bar across the window, and the other end stretched all the way down to Djeow Seow's tiny hands.

The emperor stepped to the window sill, slipped under the iron bar, saluted the gods, and slid down the rope. His robes billowed out around him like the wings of a bright kite.

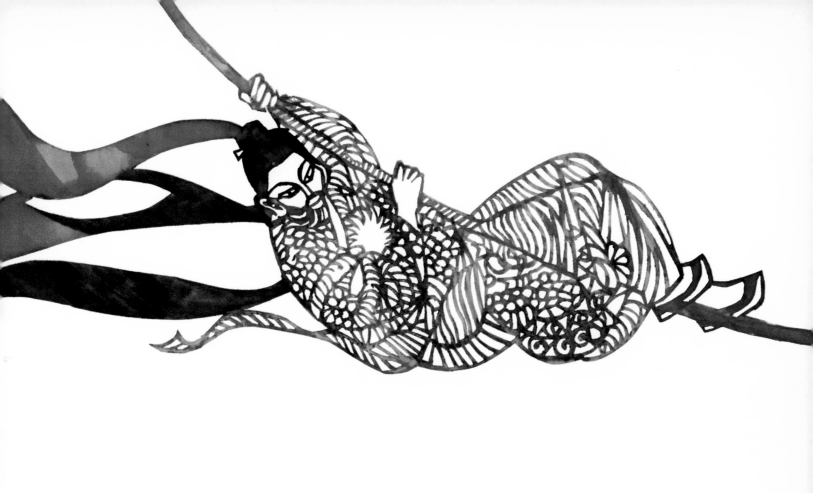

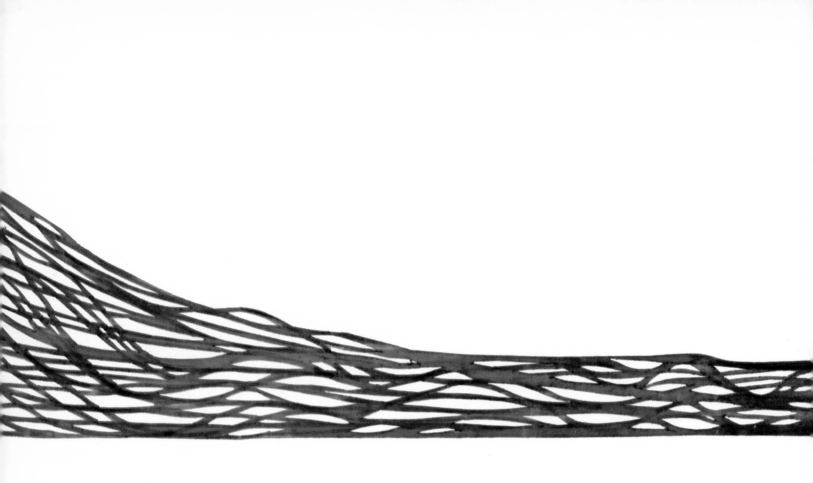

When his feet reached the ground, he knelt before his tiny daughter.
And he touched the ground before her with his lips. Then he rose
and embraced her, and she almost disappeared in his arms.

With his arm encircling her, the emperor said, "Come to thy home with me, loyal child." He lifted the tiny princess to his shoulders and carried her all the way back to the palace.

At the palace, the emperor was greeted by wild and cheering crowds.
The people were tired of the evil men, but they had been afraid to act.
With the emperor once again to guide them, they threw the plotters
into prison.

And when the other sons and daughters of the emperor heard of his return, they left off their sobbing and sighing, and they hurried home to welcome their father. But when they arrived, they were surprised to find Djeow Seow on a tiny throne by their father's side.

To the end of his days, the emperor ruled with Princess Djeow Seow close by. She never wanted for anything, especially love.

And the emperor never again neglected a person—whether great or small.

And, too, it is said that Djeow Seow ruled after him, as gentle as the wind and, in her loyalty, as unyielding.